INSTRUMENTAL PLAY-ALONG

ROCK HITS

CU00695812

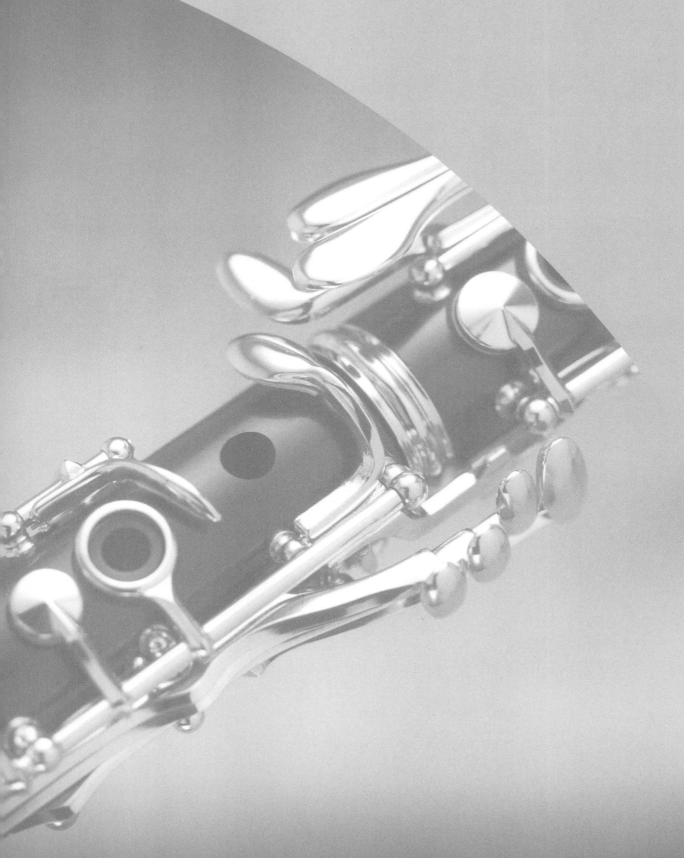

INSTRUMENTAL PLAY-ALONG

Clarinet

ROCK HITS

SOLO ARRANGEMENTS OF 15 CLASSIC SONGS WITH CD ACCOMPANIMENT

HOW TO USE THE CD ACCOMPANIMENT:
A melody cue appears on the right channel only.
If your CD player has a balance adjustment, you can adjust
the volume of the melody by turning down the right channel.

This publication is not authorised for sale in
the United States of America and/or Canada

HAL LEONARD EUROPE
DISTRIBUTED BY MUSIC SALES

Exclusive Distributors:
Music Sales Limited
14-15 Berners Street, London W1T 3LJ, UK.

Order No. HLE90002847
ISBN-13: 978-1-84609-369-2
ISBN-10: 1-84609-369-4
This book © Copyright 2007 Hal Leonard Europe

Printed in the USA

Your Guarantee of Quality
As publishers, we strive to produce every book to the highest
commercial standards. The book has been carefully designed to
minimise awkward page turns and to make playing from it a real
pleasure. Throughout, the printing and binding have been planned
to ensure a sturdy, attractive publication which should give years
of enjoyment. If your copy fails to meet our high standards,
please inform us and we will gladly replace it.

www.musicsales.com

Contents

◆ AQUALUNG

Music by IAN ANDERSON
Lyrics by JENNIE ANDERSON

CLARINET

Moderately

Electric guitar

8

BEST OF MY LOVE

Clarinet

Words and Music by JOHN DAVID SOUTHER,
DON HENLEY and GLENN FREY

❸ THE BOYS ARE BACK IN TOWN

Words and Music by
PHILIP PARRIS LYNOTT

CLARINET

BROWN EYED GIRL

Clarinet

Words and Music by
VAN MORRISON

Moderately

◆ CROCODILE ROCK

CLARINET

Words and Music by ELTON JOHN
and BERNIE TAUPIN

Light-hearted Rock

◆ DON'T STOP

CLARINET

Words and Music by
CHRISTINE McVIE

◆ 8 FREE BIRD

CLARINET

Words and Music by ALLEN COLLINS
and RONNIE VAN ZANT

◆7 FLY LIKE AN EAGLE

Clarinet

Words and Music by
STEVE MILLER

◆⑨GIMME SOME LOVIN'

Words and Music by SPENCER DAVIS,
MUFF WINWOOD and STEVE WINWOOD

Clarinet

I WANT YOU TO WANT ME

Clarinet

Words and Music by
RICK NIELSEN

LOW RIDER

Clarinet

Words and Music by SYLVESTER ALLEN, HAROLD R. BROWN,
MORRIS DICKERSON, JERRY GOLDSMITH, LEROY JORDAN,
LEE OSKAR, CHARLES W. MILLER and HOWARD SCOTT

MAGGIE MAY

Clarinet

Words and Music by ROD STEWART
and MARTIN QUITTENTON

🔶14 WALK THIS WAY

CLARINET

Words and Music by STEVEN TYLER
and JOE PERRY

WHITE WEDDING

Clarinet

Words and Music by
BILLY IDOL

🔷13 OWNER OF A LONELY HEART

Words and Music by TREVOR HORN,
JON ANDERSON, TREVOR RABIN and CHRIS SQUIRE

CLARINET

FRIEDRICH DEMNITZ

ELEMENTARY SCHOOL FOR CLARINET

ELEMENTARSCHULE FÜR KLARINETTE

EDITION PETERS

LONDON · FRANKFURT/M. · LEIPZIG · NEW YORK

INHALT / CONTENTS

ELEMENTARSCHULE FÜR KLARINETTE

von Friedrich Demnitz
(1845 – 1890)

Die ersten Übungen sollen das Hervorbringen des Tones fördern. Dazu wurde die Tonlage gewählt, in der dies am leichtesten möglich ist. Jeder Ton soll kräftig mit der Zunge angestoßen und in gleichmäßiger Stärke in vollem Wert ausgehalten werden.

I. Die einfachsten Vortragsarten
1. Tenuto

Mäßig langsames Tempo

ELEMENTARY SCHOOL FOR THE CLARINET

by Friedrich Demnitz
(1845 – 1890)

These exercises are intended to develop tone production, and for that reason those rangers have been selected in which this may most easily be accomplished. Each note must be distinctly articulated with the tongue and sustained at a constant volume for its full length.

I. The simplest forms of phrasing
1. Tenuto

The tempo always moderately slow

*)＇ Zeichen zum Atemholen

*)＇ Breathing mark

Edition Peters Nr. 2417

7209

4

6

2. Legato

Auflegen und Aufheben der Finger schnell und präzis; nur so ist eine gute Verbindung (legato) der Töne zu erreichen.

2. Legato

Finger movement must be quick and precise; only in this way can a real legato be achieved.

8

3. Staccato

Jeden Ton kräftig und kurz anstoßen

3. Staccato

Each note strong and short

9

30.10.2

4. Portamento
Langer, weicher, gebundener Stoß

4. Semi staccato

Moderato

1.

Andantino

2.

Andante con moto

3.

II. Die gebräuchlichsten dynamischen Bezeichnungen

Piano, Forte, Crescendo, Diminuendo, Forzato, Fortepiano etc.

II. The most common dynamic markings

Piano, Forte, Crescendo, Diminuendo, Forzato, Fortepiano etc.

7209

Allegro moderato

Poco adagio

III. Tonleiter Studien | III. Scale studies

1. C-Dur | 1. C major

2. a-Moll | 2. A minor

3. G-Dur | 3. G major

Andante

dolce

4. e-Moll | 4. E minor

melodisch *melodic* | harmonisch *harmonic*

Allegro energico

5. D-Dur 5. D major

Moderato

6. h-Moll 6. B minor

melodisch *melodic* harmonisch *harmonic*

Allegretto non troppo

7. A-Dur | 7. A major

Moderato assai

8. fis-Moll | 8. F♯ minor

melodisch *melodic*   harmonisch *harmonic*

Poco lento

a tempo

dolce espress.

9. E-Dur 9. E major

17

18

10. cis-Moll | 10. C# minor

11. As-Dur | 11. A♭ major

12. f-Moll | 12. F minor

13. Es-Dur | 13. E♭ major

Allegretto grazioso

14. c-Moll | 14. C minor

melodisch *melodic* | harmonisch *harmonic*

Andante con moto

15. B-Dur | 15. B♭ major

Andante con moto, quasi Allegretto

7209

16. g-Moll   16. G minor

17. F-Dur   17. F major

18. d-Moll | 18. D minor

melodisch *melodic*   harmonisch *harmonic*

Moderato

IV. Akkord Studien

1. C-Dur

IV. Arpeggio studies

1. C major

Molto moderato

2. a-Moll

Dreiklang *Triad*

2. A minor

verm. Sept. Akkord *dimin. chord of the 7th*

Andante con moto

3. F-Dur   3. F major

Dreiklang *Triad*   Dom. Sept. Akkord *Dom. chord of the 7th*

Allegretto

4. d-Moll | 4. D minor

5. B-Dur | 5. B♭ major

Dreiklang *Triad* — Dom. Sept. Akkord *Dom.chord of the 7th*

Tempo giusto leggiero

6. g-Moll
Dreiklang *Triad*

6. G minor
verm. Sept. Akkord *dimin. chord of the 7th*

Animato

7. Es-Dur

Dreiklang *Triad*

7. E♭ major

Dom. Sept. Akkord *Dom. chord of the 7th*

Alla marcia Maestoso

8. c-Moll

Dreiklang *Triad*

8. C minor

verm. Sept. Akkord dimin. chord of the 7th

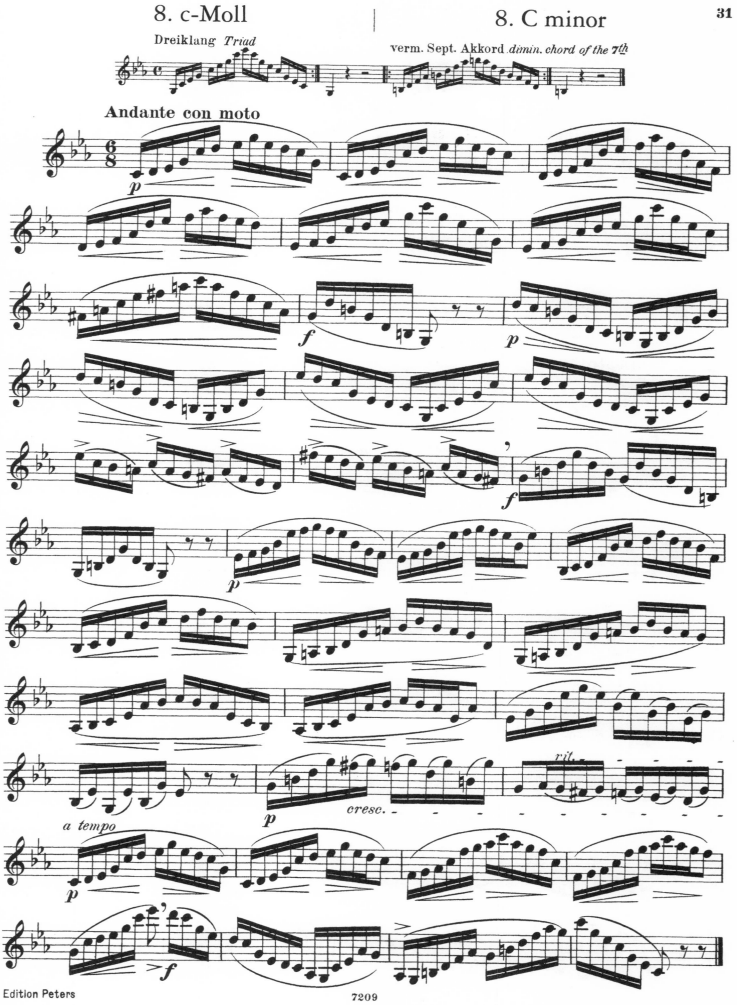

Andante con moto

9. As-Dur

Dreiklang *Triad*

9. A♭ major

Dom. Sept. Akkord *Dom. chord of the 7th*

Poco lento

Animato

Più mosso

10. f-Moll | 10. F minor

Dreiklang *Triad*

verm. Sept. Akkord *dimin. chord of the* 7th

Agitato

11. E-Dur | 11. E major

Dreiklang *Triad*   Dom. Sept. Akkord *Dom. chord of the 7th*

Allegretto commodo

12. cis-Moll | ## 12. C♯ minor

Dreiklang *Triad*   verm. Sept. Akkord *dimin. chord of the 7th*

Moderato

mp

13. A-Dur | ## 13. A major

14. fis-Moll | 14. F♯ minor

Dreiklang *Triad*

verm. Sept. Akkord. *dimin. chord of the 7th*

Moderato

rit. — — — — *, a tempo*

15. D-Dur

Dreiklang *Triad*

15. D major

Dom. Sept. Akkord Dom. chord of the 7th

Scherzo
Allegretto giocoso

16. h-Moll
Dreiklang *Triad*

16. B minor
verm. Sept. Akkord *dimin. chord of the 7th*

Allegro con fuoco

17. G-Dur | 17. G major

Dreiklang *Triad* Dom. Sept. Akkord *Dom. chord of the* 7th

Tempo commodo

18. e-Moll

18. E minor

Dreiklang *Triad*

verm. Sept. Akkord. *dimin. chord of the 7th*

Allegro

V. Die gebräuchlichsten Verzierungen

1. Kurzer Vorschlag

V. The most common ornaments

1. The acciaccatura

2. Mehrnotiger Vorschlag

2. Appogiatura of several notes

3. Doppelschlag (Mordent) | 3. The turn

4. Pralltriller | 4. The mordent

Printed by
Halstan & Co. Ltd., Amersham, Bucks, England

Solo
Début
Series

Easy Clarinet Solo Playalong Pop Hits

Wise Publications
part of The Music Sales Group
London/New York/Paris/Sydney/Copenhagen/Berlin/Madrid/Tokyo

Published by
Wise Publications
14-15 Berners Street, London W1T 3LJ, UK.

Exclusive Distributors:
Music Sales Limited
Distribution Centre, Newmarket Road, Bury St Edmunds, Suffolk IP33 3YB, UK.
Music Sales Pty Limited
120 Rothschild Avenue, Rosebery, NSW 2018, Australia.

Order No. AM990187
ISBN 978-1-84772-042-9
This book © Copyright 2007 Wise Publications,
a division of Music Sales Limited.

Arranging and engraving supplied by Camden Music.
Compiled by Heather Slater.
Printed in the EU.

CD recorded, mixed and mastered by John Rose and Jonas Persson.
Instrumental solos by Jamie Talbot.
New backing tracks arranged by Camden Music.
Backing tracks: 'Crazy' arranged by Danny Gluckstein;
'Patience' and 'You Give Me Something' arranged by John Maul.
Melody line arrangements by Christopher Hussey.

Your Guarantee of Quality
As publishers, we strive to produce every book to the highest commercial standards.
The music has been freshly engraved and the book has been carefully designed to minimise
awkward page turns and to make playing from it a real pleasure.
Particular care has been given to specifying acid-free, neutral-sized paper made from pulps
which have not been elemental chlorine bleached. This pulp is from farmed sustainable forests
and was produced with special regard for the environment.
Throughout, the printing and binding have been planned to ensure a sturdy, attractive
publication which should give years of enjoyment.
If your copy fails to meet our high standards, please inform us and we will gladly replace it.

www.musicsales.com

FREE bonus material downloadable to your computer.
Visit: www.hybridpublications.com
Registration is free and easy.
Your registration code is: NC391

Clarinet
Fingering Chart

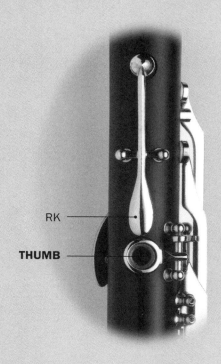

RK

THUMB

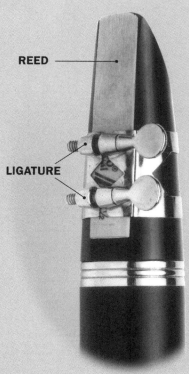

REED

LIGATURE

Mouthpiece

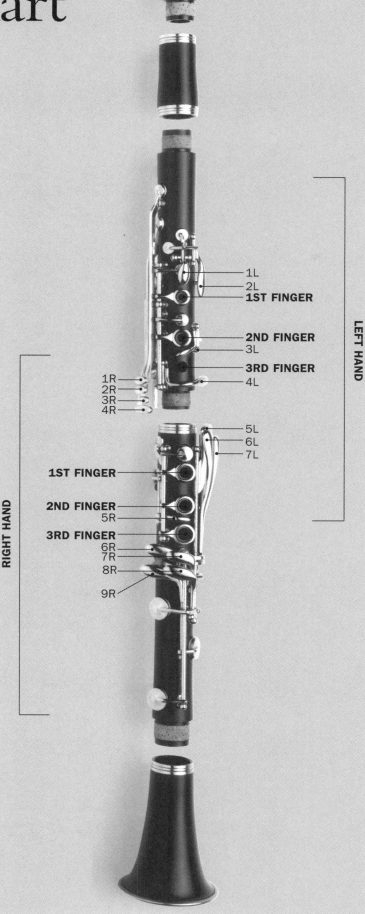

1L
2L
1ST FINGER

2ND FINGER
3L

3RD FINGER
4L

1R
2R
3R
4R

LEFT HAND

RIGHT HAND

5L
6L
7L

1ST FINGER

2ND FINGER
5R

3RD FINGER
6R
7R
8R

9R

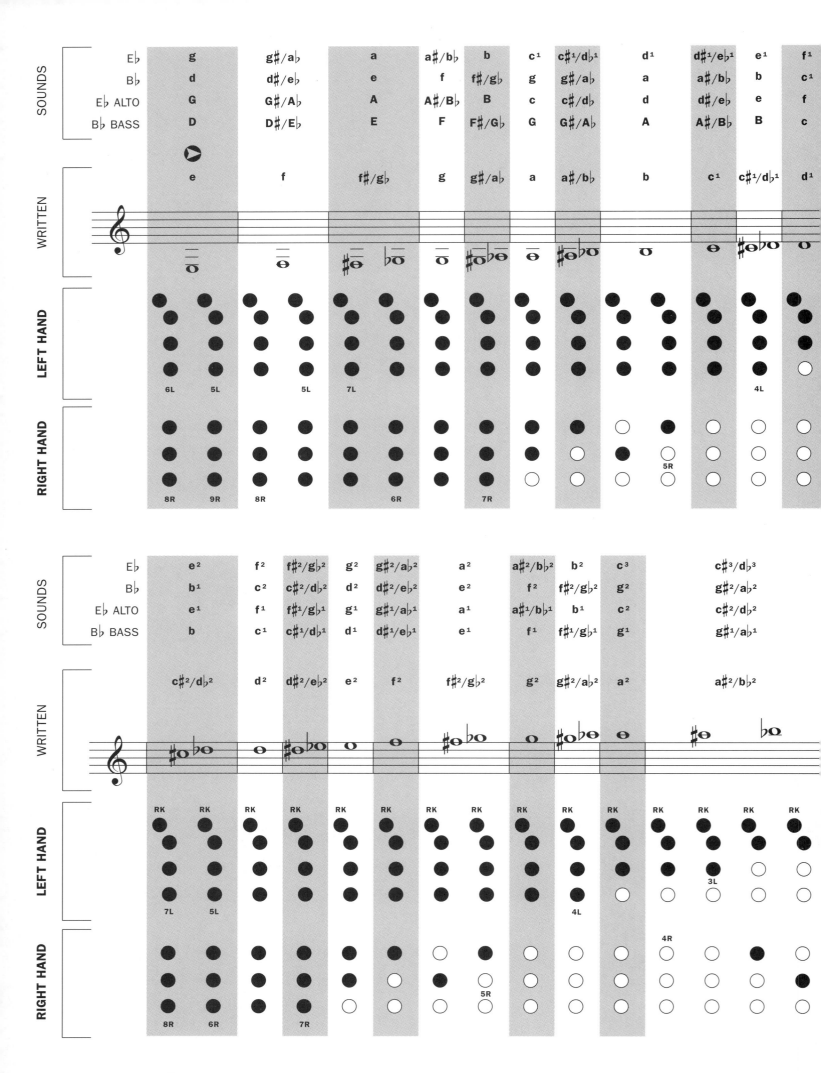

Indicates the lower limit of the best playing range for E♭, B♭, E♭ Alto and B♭ Bass Clarinets

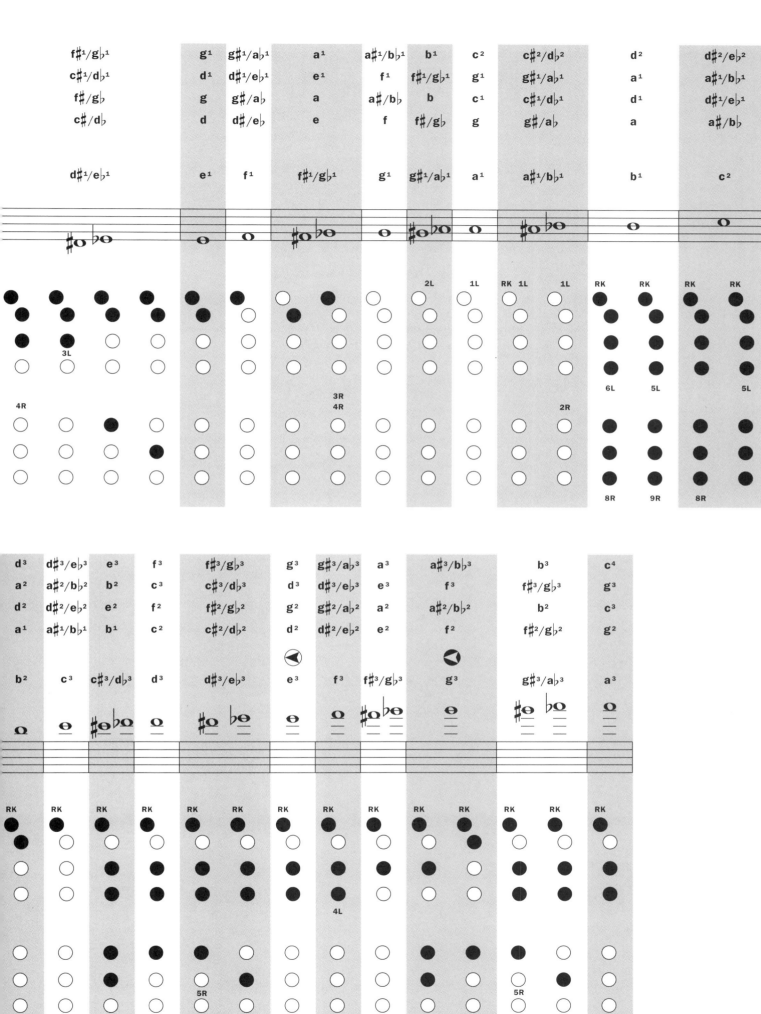

PERFORMANCE TIPS

Welcome to this exciting collection of playalong songs, featuring some of your favourite pop hits!

Before you begin to play, make sure your instrument is in tune
(there are tuning notes on Track 1 of the CD) and listen to the demonstration performances
on Tracks 2–11 while following along with the music.

Throughout the book, you'll notice some tiny notes written into the music—these are called **cues,**
and they are not to be played. They show you what is happening on the backing track
(i.e. what the other instruments are playing) so that you will know when to come in.

There are lots of tricky semiquaver rhythms to watch out for—but don't worry,
they are much easier than they look! If you listen to original recordings of the songs
and the demonstration performances on the CD, you will get a good idea
of how they should sound and they will feel more natural to play.

Remember: always practise the passages that you find difficult on their own,
playing them slowly, but still keeping in time.

Below are some suggestions that will help you improve your performance,
including practice tips, handy 'shortcuts' to simplify the music while you are learning it,
and some hints that will make it easier to fit your performance to the CD accompaniment.

LEAVE RIGHT NOW (Will Young)

- There are some tricky rhythms to master in this song—you will find it easier if you practise each phrase on its own, and then gradually put the song together phrase-by-phrase.

- The slurs that appear throughout help to make the melody flow, and will improve the sound of your performance. However, while you are learning the song, it might help you to leave the slurs out to begin with, until you are confident with the rhythms. Try practising the opening of the first verse without slurs:

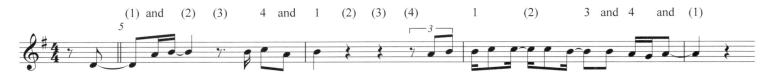

Now try playing the same passage with the slurs:

- Before you put the whole song together, make sure you understand the repeat scheme. **D.S. al Coda** at the end of bar 36 indicates that you should go back to the sign 𝄋 (bar 17) and play up to the end of bar 22, where you will see the sign **to Coda** ⊕. When you reach the **to Coda** ⊕ sign, jump to the ⊕ **Coda** section at bar 37.

CRAZY (Gnarls Barkley)

- There are lots of tricky semiquaver rhythms in this song, so once again practise each phrase on its own, slowly, before you put the whole song together.

- Notice that there are a number of **articulation marks** in this arrangement, which give character to the melody. There are **staccato** dots (indicating that these notes should be shorter than their written note length and tongued) and also **marcato** symbols (∧) which indicate that the notes should be 'marked' (accented) and played slightly shorter than their written duration (but not as short as a staccato). Practise the phrase below in order to master the different articulations:

- An important feature of the chorus is **syncopation**. A syncopated rhythm occurs when beats of the bar which are normally unaccented are given an accent. Practise the opening phrase of the chorus, counting very carefully:

The syncopations occur on the 'and' of the 4th beat of bar 17 and the 'and' of the 2nd beat of bar 18 (and then similarly in bars 19 and 20), beats which would normally be unaccented.

- Watch out for the **accidentals**, for example the G♯s in bar 13, and particularly the accidentals in the last line of the music—these become natural again later in the same bar.

- Make sure you understand what the **1st time bar** and **2nd time bar** symbols tell you to do—be prepared to repeat from bar 26, and go straight to the '2nd time bar' after the second time through.

DON'T CHA (Pussycat Dolls)

- The little lines above the notes, for example in bars 9, 10 and 14, are called **tenuto** marks. These indicate that you should hold these notes for their full written duration and tongue them slightly more than you would normally, so that they are slightly accented.

- This is a simple tune, but be aware of the **syncopation** in the verse section—the slurs and ties mean that many of the strong beats are not tongued:

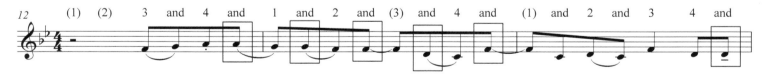

- By contrast, the chorus (beginning at bar 25) is not syncopated and should be played with confidence and bounce, which you can achieve by making the **staccato** notes shorter than their written duration.

- Make sure you understand the repeat scheme of this song: when you reach the end of the **1st time bar** in bar 40, go back to the repeat sign in bar 9 and play on, this time missing out the '1st time bar' and jumping to the **2nd time bar**. At the end of this section, **D.S. al Fine** tells you to go back to the sign 𝄋 (bar 9) and play up to the end of bar 39, where **Fine** indicates the end of the song.

- Also, notice the instruction 'On 𝄋 fade to end' in bar 33—when you play this section for the last time (on the repeat from the sign 𝄋) start fading in volume from this point until the end of the song.

FIX YOU (Coldplay)

- Look carefully at the first three phrases in this song. You will notice that they use almost the same notes, but have slightly different rhythms:

- Also have a look at the phrase from the 4th beat of bar 12 through to the double barline at the end of bar 20—it is very similar to what you have already played, with a few little changes to the notes and rhythms. Spotting similarities between phrases in music will help to make the task of learning a new piece easier.

- Now practise the first two-bar phrase of the refrain, bars 21–23, and notice that this phrase is repeated immediately in bars 23 to 25:

IS IT ANY WONDER? (Keane)

- Watch out for the assortment of articulation marks: there are **staccato**, **tenuto** and **accent** marks to think about. While you are learning the tune, don't worry about the articulation to begin with—then, once you are more familiar with the piece, try adding it to improve the character of your performance. Practise the phrase below to help you master the difference between a staccato and a tenuto mark:

- The instruction 'cresc. poco a poco' in this passage tells you to gradually get louder until you reach the end of bar 25.

- The rhythms in this song are quite straightforward, but it is worth practising bars 30 and 31 in order to master the articulation and the quick semiquaver-dotted quaver rhythm on beat 4:

- There aren't very many long rests in this piece, so the ticks ✓ indicate suitable places for taking a breath.

PATIENCE (Take That)

- This song features fast semiquaver rhythms. Practise them slowly to begin with and leave out the slurs, until you are confident enough to reintroduce the slurring. Try the opening phrases below in this way, counting very carefully to make sure you keep in time, and once you have mastered it, add in the slurs:

- Have a look at the repeat scheme before you start to play, so that you know how to follow the score. **D.S. al Coda** at the end of bar 34 indicates that you should go back to the sign 𝄋 (bar 15) and play until you reach the **to Coda** ⊕ sign (at the end of bar 22). Once you have played bar 22, go straight to the ⊕ **Coda** section at bar 35.

- Watch out for the **accidentals** in the first line of the Coda (bars 35 to 37).

SOMETHING BEAUTIFUL (Robbie Williams)

- The rhythms in this song are mainly simple quaver patterns, although there are a few trickier semiquaver bits and some **syncopated** rhythms to look out for. Practise the passage below, which includes examples of both of these, and count very carefully so that you keep in time:

The notes in boxes are syncopated—that is, they are accented beats that would normally be unaccented.

- Watch out for the **accidental** G♮s in bars 11 and 15, and the **cautionary accidentals** (the bracketed sharps) before the Gs in the bars that immediately follow, which indicate that the Gs should be sharp again, as in the key signature. Also watch out for the **accidental** C♮ in bar 33.

- There is an assortment of articulation marks in the refrain, which begins on the upbeat into bar 19—there are **staccato**, **accent** and **tenuto** marks to help give the tune character. Practise the phrase below to help you master the different types of articulation:

- Notice that the second half of the refrain (upbeat into bars 27 to 34) is very similar to the first half (as above).

- In bar 43 the song changes from E major to F major (modulating up a semitone)—remember that all Fs, Cs, Gs and Ds are no longer sharp and that now all Bs are flat. In addition, there are a few accidentals to watch out for in this section!

- The last note of the song, F, should be held for a few beats longer than its written duration, as it has a **fermata** ⌢ (pause mark) above it.

THIS LOVE (Maroon 5)

- In verse 1 (bars 9–16) and verse 2 (bars 29–36) of this song, the notes don't move very much—however, the rhythms are quite tricky. Have a listen to the demonstration performance on the CD and the original song to get an idea of how it is supposed to sound. Then practise each phrase slowly, counting very carefully, until the rhythms feel more natural to play. The first four bars of verse 1 contain most of the rhythms you'll need to know, so start by practising this passage:

- The chorus, which begins in bar 17, is marked **_f_** (forte) indicating that it should be played loudly, and also *'pesante'*, which means heavily.

- In the second verse (bars 29 to 36) there are not many opportunities to take a breath, so the ticks ✓ indicate suitable places to catch a quick gasp!

UNFAITHFUL (Rihanna)

- There are lots of semiquavers in this song, which might make it look a little scary at first, but there are not too many syncopated rhythms—once you've got the idea of how it goes, it won't be as hard as it looks!

- Practise the following phrase (the upbeat into bars 13 to 16), which does include some syncopation:

- The section from the upbeat into bar 27 to the middle of bar 38 is the second verse. If you compare it to the first verse (bar 5 to the middle of bar 16) you'll notice that it is very similar with a few added notes. Similarly, if you take a look at the last chorus (bar 48 to the middle of bar 55) you'll notice that the beginning resembles that of the first chorus (bars 17 to 24).

YOU GIVE ME SOMETHING (James Morrison)

- Practise this song phrase-by-phrase to make sure you get all of the semiquaver rhythms correct. Listen to the demonstration performance on the CD and the original song to give you a good idea of how the tune should sound.

- Try the opening four bars of the tune without the slurring (as below) and once you have mastered the rhythms add the slurs back in:

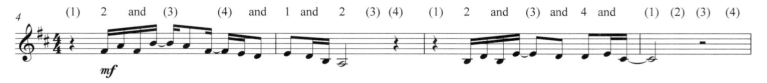

- Before you begin to play the whole song, check that you're familiar with the repeat scheme—locate where the **1st** and **2nd time bars** are, and note which passages you will need to repeat.

- In bars 42 to 43, the same three-note pattern is played three times, with slightly different rhythms. The second entry is marked *'like an echo'*, so get gradually quieter and more distant.

Leave Right Now
(Will Young)

Words & Music by Francis White

12

Crazy

(Gnarls Barkley)

Words & Music by Thomas Callaway, Brian Burton, Gianfranco Reverberi & Gian Piero Reverberi

15

Don't Cha
(Pussycat Dolls)

Words & Music by Thomas Callaway & Anthony Ray

With attitude! ♩ = 120

On $\%$ fade to end

Fine

D.S. al Fine

Fix You

(Coldplay)

Words & Music by Guy Berryman, Chris Martin, Jon Buckland & Will Champion

Is It Any Wonder?
(Keane)

Words & Music by Richard Hughes, James Sanger, Tim Rice-Oxley & Tom Chaplin

Patience

(Take That)

Words & Music by Mark Owen, Gary Barlow, John Shanks, Jason Orange & Howard Donald

Something Beautiful

(Robbie Williams)

Words & Music by Robbie Williams & Guy Chambers

This Love
(Maroon 5)

Words & Music by Adam Levine, James Valentine, Jesse Carmichael, Mickey Madden & Ryan Dusick

Unfaithful

(Rihanna)

Words & Music by Mikkel Eriksen, Tor Erik Hermansen & Shaffer Smith

You Give Me Something
(James Morrison)

Words & Music by Francis White & James Morrison

CD Track Listing

1 Tuning notes

Full instrumental performances...

2 Leave Right Now **Will Young**
(White) Universal Music Publishing Limited.

3 Crazy **Gnarls Barkley**
(Callaway/Burton/Reverberi/Reverberi)
Chrysalis Music Limited/Warner/Chappell Music Publishing/Atmosphere Music Limited.

4 Don't Cha **Pussycat Dolls**
(Callaway/Ray) Notting Hill Music (UK) Limited.

5 Fix You **Coldplay**
(Berryman/Martin/Buckland/Champion) BMG Music Publishing Limited.

6 Is It Any Wonder? **Keane**
(Hughes/Sanger/Rice-Oxley/Chaplin) BMG Music Publishing Limited.

7 Patience **Take That**
(Owen/Barlow/Shanks/Orange/Donald)
EMI Music Publishing Limited/Warner/Chappell Music North America/Sony
/ATV Music Publishing (UK) Limited/BMG Music Publishing Limited.

8 Something Beautiful **Robbie Williams**
(Williams/Chambers) BMG Music Publishing Limited/EMI Music Publishing Limited.

9 This Love **Maroon 5**
(Levine/Valentine/Carmichael/Madden/Dusick) BMG Music Publishing Limited.

10 Unfaithful **Rihanna**
(Eriksen/Hermansen/Smith)
Zomba Music Publishers Limited/Sony/ATV Music Publishing (UK) Limited/EMI Music Publishing Limited.

11 You Give Me Something **James Morrison**
(White/Morrison) Sony/ATV Music Publishing (UK) Limited/Universal Music Publishing Limited.

Backing tracks only...

12 Leave Right Now **Will Young**
13 Crazy **Gnarls Barkley**
14 Don't Cha **Pussycat Dolls**
15 Fix You **Coldplay**
16 Is It Any Wonder? **Keane**
17 Patience **Take That**
18 Something Beautiful **Robbie Williams**
19 This Love **Maroon 5**
20 Unfaithful **Rihanna**
21 You Give Me Something **James Morrison**

**To remove your CD from the plastic sleeve, lift the small lip to break the perforations.
Replace the disc after use for convenient storage.**